The Heeler

stories

Russell Hill

[signature: Russell Hill]

Blackfox Press   Fairfax, California

Blackfox Press
P.O. Box 432
Fairfax California 94978-0432

First Edition

ISBN: 0-9725763-1-2

Library of Congress Control Number: 2005929789

Cover photograph: Maya, Rio Dell: Russell Hill
Author photograph: Eleanor Leith Hill
Layout and Design: DIMI PRESS, Salem, Oregon

For Eleanor with love from R

The Heeler

The highway from Grass Valley to Marysville comes down out of the Sierras in long, looping curves, descending quickly like a chute spilling out into the Central Valley and he kept a steady speed, sixty miles an hour, looking back at the jacked-up pickup that was tailing him, waiting for a passing lane so the asshole could move ahead. But he grew tired of the grill looming large in his rear view mirror and at the next turnout he pulled over and the truck roared past. He pulled back onto the road and watched the truck grow smaller. It was hot and there was no AC in his truck so the window was down, the wind whipping his hair. Leaning forward, his sweat-soaked shirt peeled from the seat back and he let it dry before pressing back against the sudden chill. He dipped his hand into the open cooler on the seat next to him, held his hand among the melting ice cubes, and ran it over his face, feeling the wind evaporate the cold water. Ahead the sun was settling over the coastal range and the hills were burnished brown, wheat-colored, rocks sticking up in the fields, the trees stunted by the endless sun. When the road began to level out into the valley he passed a fruit stand and on a whim pulled to the side, waited for the cars that followed him to drive on, and then made a u-turn, his truck tires crunching on the gravel on the far side of the road, driving back the 500 yards to the narrow apron in front of the stand. There were firm tomatoes and sweet corn with the tassels still green and an old man who said, "How you doin' pardner? Hot enough?" and he filled a plastic bag with tomatoes and corn and peaches. The old man weighed his purchase and said, "Four ninety," and he thought, at home at the farmers market it would be ten dollars. He took one of the tomatoes and bit into it, the juice squirting onto his chin.

"That's the best way," the old man said. "Not many people do that, you know."

"Do what?"

"Eat a tomato like that. Best taste in the whole world."

"I used to pick tomatoes with my great aunt when I was a kid. She canned them."

`"My wife does that."

"When we picked tomatoes our hands got all black and she taught my brother and me to wash our hands with a green tomato, smash it up and scrub our hands. They came out clean as a whistle." He wasn't sure why he was telling this stranger about his childhood. The heat crackled and he suddenly realized there was a dog at the old man's feet, limp, lying on the cement floor and the only thing that indicated it was alive were the eyes that stared at him, moving slightly when it shifted its body.

Back in the truck he waited until the road was clear, turned west again and accelerated to stay ahead of the cars that grew large in his side view mirror. A few miles down the road the cars in front of him were slowed, brake lights lit, and when he pulled in behind the last car he could see a cop coming back, bending to say something into the driver's window of each car, then moving on.

There were yellow and red lights flashing beyond the cop's car in the middle of the road, an accident ahead. The cars were turning and heading back the way he had come and he thought, oh shit, they're detouring around the accident. No telling how far back we'll have to go. The cop waved at him, circling his arm in the air, motioning him to follow the other cars.

He turned onto the shoulder because the turning radius of the Dodge was wide and that was when he saw the dog. It came toward him almost sideways, running as if it were escaping from someone and he stopped the truck, watched it, and then the cop came toward him.

"Move it!" the cop shouted. "Follow those cars!" pointing back toward where he had come from and the dog paused in the field, looking one way, then another, and he realized the dog had a big splotch of blood on its back and the back of its head. It stopped, confused, at the edge of the field opposite the truck. He leaned across the seat, popped the latch and the door swung open. He called to the dog several times, gave a shrill whistle and the dog turned, looking at the truck, then back again at the blinking lights.

"Hey!" the cop shouted, closer now, obviously pissed off.

He opened the driver's door and stepped out, going around the front of the truck to face the dog. It backed up a bit, and it was shaking, the blood on its back glittering in the afternoon sun. He spoke reassuringly, approaching it slowly, conscious of the shouting cop on the other side of the truck and then he had his hand cupped around the dog's collar and he reached under the dog's belly and scooped it up, holding it close to his chest. He was aware that he was doing a stupid thing. If the dog were injured it might very well bite him and he tried to keep the head under his arm as he slid the dog onto the seat next to the cooler. By now the cop was at the truck.

"What the hell is wrong with you, buddy? You deaf or something?"

"The dog," he said, pointing to it. "It may be hurt."

The cop looked at the dog, then back at the accident.

"Well, you're sure as hell not going up there. It's a mess. Turn around with the others. The detour will drop you off just in front of the accident. Jesus," he added, his voice softening. "He's the only one left."

He checked the dog when he got back into the truck but he couldn't find any injury. The blood wasn't the dog's blood, that was for sure. The dog continued to shake and he took his old sweatshirt from behind the seat and wrapped it around the dog.It was not a big dog, short-haired and he guessed it was mostly heeler, a cow dog, but there was some sheepdog mixed in, too, because the coat was a mottled black and white. He remembered dogs like that from his childhood on the ranch. They rode in the back of his father's truck and slept outside on the lean-to porch, but the ranch was long gone and so were his father and the dogs. I'm older than my father, he thought. In dog years, those dogs would be about 300 years old.

"Not you," he said to the dog on the seat beside him. The dog raised its head at the sound of his voice.

"You're still a kid, even in dog years. Anybody under fifty is a kid."

He turned back toward Grass Valley, following the cars that had been diverted and a mile later the traffic began to slow. Ahead of him the line of cars was turning off to the south and there was a steady stream of cars coming from the opposite direction, diverted from the other end of the accident. He turned off the highway onto the narrow road and now he was passing the occasional isolated shack, then a half-finished house that looked like it had been abandoned in mid-construction, and he wondered what it would be like to live out here among the scrub oaks, surrounded by abandoned cars. Another half mile and the line of cars turned again, this time west, and within a few minutes he had reached the highway where two police cars waited, lights pulsing, two stocky cops waving the cars onto the main road. Off to the right he could see a tow truck with the jacked-up pickup that had passed him, windshield shattered, front end buckled under, a door roped closed. On the other side of the road was an old van, the front end crushed, and there were two paramedic vans in the middle of the road and more cops.

"Dumb son of a bitch," he muttered. "I shouldn't have let him pass me," but he knew that the pickup would have passed him anyway, even if it meant going over the double line. He wondered if the dog had come from the pickup or the van. The first cop had said something about the dog being the only survivor.

He pulled past the cops and off onto the shoulder. One of the cops turned and waved to him to keep going and when he didn't move, the cop came toward the truck, still waving insistently toward Marysville.

"Keep going," he called out. "There's nothing to see."

"I've got a dog here and I think he belongs to someone in that wreck."

The cop came up to the side of the truck , looked in.

"I picked him up on the other side, where the other cop is. He came running from here and he's all bloody."

"I'll call animal control," the cop said. "You stay right here."

"Hold on," he said. "There's no point in sending him to the pound. Can't we find out who he belongs to?"

"Not now. There's nobody here who can tell you. You stay right here and I'll give them a call. It may take a while for them to get here, though."

He thought briefly about what would happen: a truck would come and take the frightened animal to the pound where it would go into a cage and if the cop was right, maybe nobody would come to claim it.

"How about if I just hang onto the dog? Give you my name and come back to Marysville tomorrow and see if we can find out who it belongs to?"

The cop studied him. "Suit yourself," he said. "Is it hurt?"

"I don't think so. It's not his blood."

"Some ID?" The cop reached out his hand.

He took out his wallet, fished out his driver's license and the cop wrote down his name and license number on a note pad. "Give us a call tomorrow," the cop said, turning back toward the line of cars.

The tow truck with the pickup went by, and there was no doubt that it was the same truck that had passed him an hour before. He tried to remember what the driver looked like but he hadn't seen the driver, only the grill and the hood in his rear view mirror and the side of the truck as it roared past and then the black outline of the driver's head and shoulders as it receded on the road. Had the dog been in the truck? He didn't remember seeing it. An hour ago there had been a man in that truck, alive, anxious to get somewhere, maybe looking for a cold beer or a wife at home or maybe he was the kind of person who was always in a hurry, swore at slow drivers, pumped the accelerator at stop lights. Now the man was dead, gone, no longer breathing, snuffed out, and he thought of a candle on the table on his back porch with the evening wind rising, suddenly flickering and it was out with an errant puff of wind; instead of driving along a two-lane road toward the black   outline of the Sutter Buttes, the sun gone, the fields a soft sienna, the man was an inert body on a gurney in the back of an ambulance. In his memory, the side of the truck passing him was sharp, the truck body raised above the big tires, as if he had re-wound the film, was again watching the living man's head and shoulders grow smaller as the truck disappeared on the road ahead and it struck him that the man had grown smaller and smaller until his life had disappeared. He remembered the exercise that Mrs. Sterns, his junior high school art teacher had made them draw: an object on one side of the paper, and lines diminishing to an imaginary point on the opposite edge of the paper and another rendition of the same object, this one smaller, and another, tiny, near what she called the vanishing point. He remembered a girl who had drawn a picture of Mrs. Sterns, repeating it, making her smaller and smaller until she disappeared, and Mrs. Sterns praised her work, unaware that the girl's picture was a cruel joke in which the art teacher and her rigid set of drawing rules vanished forever.

He looked over at the dog and wondered if the dog had any thoughts. Had he traded one truck for another, one man for another? Were men and trucks interchangeable in the dog's world?

"What about it," he said. "Were you in that truck? Or in the van?" The dog looked up at the sound of his voice. He reached out to rub the dog's head. The dog withdrew, pulling back toward the door.

"That's OK," he said. "You've had a bad day. I'll shut up and leave you alone."

He concentrated on driving, the light failing now, and he knew his night vision wasn't good. The glaucoma meant that his peripheral vision was going and he no longer trusted himself after dark. It would be good to get home.. He looked at his watch, held his wrist close to his face and he could see that it was almost seven. The light was going quicker now, and with it the air was cooler. The windshield was dotted with the remains of rice bugs, clouds of them coming out at dusk from the rice fields on both sides of the highway.

It was dark when he pulled into the long gravel driveway that led to the house. It was an isolated farmhouse, something he could afford to rent, far out from town, and when he stopped the truck there was silence. He waited, listening to the cracking of the cooling engine, and then he got out of the truck, went around to the other door and opened it. He lifted the sweatshirt from the dog and called to it.

"Come on, boy," he said, moving back toward the house. The dog watched him, shifted, and dropped out of the truck. It followed him onto the porch where he opened the door, held the screen so the dog could follow him in. The dog hesitated, then came into the front room. It was still hot inside the house and he opened the windows, pulled the chain on the ancient ceiling fan and it hummed to life.

He went into the bathroom, ran a few inches of water into the tub and called the dog again. It followed him and he hoisted it into the tub, scooping water onto its back. The water in the tub turned red, and he soaped the dog, scrubbing the dried blood from its fur. It stood in the tub, legs braced, looking straight ahead, while he rinsed it off, pulled the plug and watched the red water swirl down the drain.

He took his towel from the rack and rubbed the dog. It shook itself and he lifted it out of the tub.

"There," he said. Then he added, "You're OK now. I

drive slow. You'll probably outlive me."

He went into the kitchen and took a cold beer from the refrigerator, came back onto the front porch and lowered himself into the old chair that was against the wall.

The dog went to the edge of the porch and folded itself so that it could look up the driveway, as if it were waiting for someone, head resting on its paws.

But the mosquitoes from the rice fields were fierce and they went back inside where he boiled some water, dropped an ear of corn into the pot, chopped up the tomatoes with some basil and olive oil. He fished out the corn, slathered margarine over it, and that was his supper. Then he realized the dog hadn't eaten and when he looked in the refrigerator there wasn't much that a dog would like, so they went out to the pickup and he drove into town, pulling into the drive-in lane at the Jack-in-the-Box. At the loudspeaker he told the girl he wanted two Jumbo Jacks, meat only, no sauce, just the buns and the meat. Then he pulled into the parking lot, unwrapped the burgers and put them on the floor where the dog swallowed them in several gulps.

"Still hungry?" he asked

The dog didn't answer.

He drove back around through the lane and ordered another Jumbo Jack, and then, as an afterthought, a vanilla milkshake. He could imagine his wife raising her eyebrows at that.

"It's for the dog," he said out loud, as if she were there on the seat next to the dog. She only raised her eyebrows again in disapproval and he said, "OK, it's for me. One freaking milkshake isn't going to kill me."

The dog ate the burger more slowly this time, leaving half the bun on the floor of the truck and he drove down the main street in the warm night air, sipping at the waxy milkshake container. The milkshake was too sweet, cloying, and he poured the rest of it out the window.

At the stop light he turned to the dog and asked, "You want a beer?"

"Of course it doesn't want a beer," his wife said.

"How would you know? You're dead. You've been dead for two years. You weren't there this afternoon when I found him."

"It's not good for dogs to drink alcohol. And, for that matter, it's not good for you, either."

"Ignore her," he said to the dog.

"Terrific," said his wife. "That's what you did for 45 years. You only pretended to listen."

"I asked you, you want a beer?" he said to the dog.

It raised its head and looked at him. The light had changed.

"No answer. I'll take that as a yes," he said.

He turned left toward the foothills, drove a block, and stopped in front of a low cinder block building with a flickering neon BAR on the roof.

"Come on," he said to the dog. The dog came across the seat and dropped to the ground.

"You're going to smell like beer and cigarettes," she said.

"Don't start in on me. You can't smell anything any more. It must be a great relief."

"I'm not the only one who could smell you," she said. "Your daughter used to complain to me all the time."

"My daughter is forty years old, has two kids and lives in Iowa," he said. "Compared to a messy diaper, I probably smell sweet."

He pushed open the door and went into the dark interior. Two men at the bar turned, and one of them said, "You ever hear the joke that starts, 'an old man and a dog came into a bar?'"

"No," he said, "but I heard the one about the two morons drinking beer on a Friday night." He slid onto a stool. The dog waited beside him

"Where'd you get the dog, Rollie?" the man asked.

"I believe he's a gift," Rollie said.

"What do you mean, you believe he's a gift?"

"Just that. There was a whole line of trucks and cars and

he came to mine. Just like that. He selected me."

"On purpose?

"No, you might say it was an accident." Rollie slid two dollar bills across the bar. "Draw me a red beer, Ray."

The bartender drew a glass of draft, reached under the bar, brought up a can of tomato juice and poured a slug into the beer.

"Why in hell do you ruin perfectly good beer like that, Rollie?" the man asked.

"It's a nod to my wife, Charlie. Vitamin C and vitamin A. This makes it a health food drink."

"If you don't mind my saying so, you lost your wife two years ago, Rollie."

"I didn't lose her, Charlie. I have a remarkable sense of direction. Sometimes she might have lost me, but I never lost her. She died."

"Exactly my point. I don't think she's looking over your shoulder."

"You'd be surprised," Rollie said. He looked down the bar past the two men where his wife sat, her nose wrinkled, grimacing, he guessed, at the smell of beer and cigarettes.

"So where'd the dog come from?"

"Out on 20, the other side of Marysville." He told the story of the truck passing him, the dog coming through the field with blood on its back and when he had finished, Charlie said, "Holy shit, Rollie. It was the same asshole who passed you?"

He nodded.

"And the cop said you could keep him?"

"No, tomorrow I've got to go back over to Marysville and find out if he belongs to somebody. But tonight he's drinking with me."

Rollie had two beers while the dog lay at the foot of the bar stool and then drove back to the house. There was no sign of his wife and he told the dog, "she's pissed off that I took you to Ray's. And after two beers she'd say, 'you're not driving. The last thing we need is a DUI.' But now she can't drive, so we're on our own." He stopped at the 7-11, bought a carton of eggs and some frozen sausages.

"You like sausage and eggs?" he asked the dog. "Me, I'm supposed to eat fake eggs. Fake sausage, too. But tomorrow we're going to celebrate. You may disappear on me tomorrow." He wished he had not stopped at the intersection and he wished the second cop hadn't taken his ID, but the dog might belong to someone and one thing he hadn't turned into in his old age was a dog thief.

He fixed a bed for the dog out of old blankets and once, during the night, he woke to hear the dog wandering the house, its nails clicking on the floor. He got up, went to the door, let the dog out and waited while it took a leak. It was cool now, the mosquitoes gone, stars out, and somewhere he could hear a train.

The next morning he scrambled half a dozen eggs and all of the sausage, sat out on the porch with his plate on his lap while the dog ate from a plate of scrambled eggs and sausage on the floor. His wife stood by the railing. "That's my Spode," she said. "You're feeding a stray dog with my Spode."

"You'll notice he's not using a knife and fork. Just his tongue. I doubt if he can chip it with his tongue."

"You've got a smart answer for everything," she said. "I wanted those dishes to go to our daughter."

"She's in Iowa, the dishes are here. She can have them any time she wants."

"You could visit her."

"It wouldn't be the same without you. End of discussion."

Rollie took the dog's dish from the floor. "Nice job," he said. "Clean as a whistle."

It was beginning to heat up when he pulled out of the driveway and he knew it would be another scorcher by noon. He drove the 40 minutes to Marysville and found the police station. He explained to the sergeant who he was and the sergeant talked to someone and then someone else and eventually the same cop who had taken his name appeared.

"Good of you to come back, Mr. Decker. You've still got that dog?"

Shit, Rollie thought, he didn't expect me to come back. I could have been home free.

"He's out in my truck."

"It belonged to the driver of the pickup."

"What happened?"

"He went over the line to pass, and a Mexican who worked for a rice farmer came onto the road about the same time. Neither one of them had a chance. The dog must of been thrown clear. How he survived without injury is a miracle. You're sure he isn't hurt?"

"He doesn't appear to be"

The cop looked at his notebook and said, "Next of kin is a woman in Live Oak. Apparently she's not his wife. I can give you her address."

"I'd appreciate it."

The cop went to a computer terminal, typed in something and came back with a printout. "Her name's Helena Norris. You want me to call her, tell her you've got the dog?"

"No, I'll go over myself."

"You know where Live Oak is?"

"I did a job there once. I've been through it on 99 a dozen times. I can find it."

He went back out to the truck. He sat for a few minutes, then turned to the dog and said, "What I'm hoping is that this lady doesn't want you."

"You couldn't wait for me to die so you could get yourself a new dog," his wife said. She was sitting on the seat next to the window, with the dog between them.

"We had a dog when you were alive."

"Quincy was never high on your list, Rollie. You might remember you used to call him names like Himmler and Hitler."

"He was a schnauzer, a regular little brown shirt dog. Little dog complex. You may remember that we couldn't trust him around the children."

"That was your fault."

"If you're referring to the fact that I drop-kicked the little bastard every time he bit me, I plead guilty. But you might also remember that I was the one who walked him, and when he'd bit every groomer in the county I was the one who muzzled him and clipped him. Give me a little credit here, Elaine."

"You couldn't wait until he died. And now you're going to get yourself the kind of dog you always wanted."

"And this bothers you?"

"You know I can't stand big dogs."

"He's not a big dog. He's a medium sized dog."

"He's big enough."

"What I want is a dog that will sit in my truck and look out the window and when I'm out of the truck he'll sit in the driver's seat and pretend he's driving."

"Rollie, that's nonsense!"

Rollie looked at the dog. "Can you drive?" he asked. "Or at least pretend to drive?"

The dog raised its head and looked at him.

"No answer. I'll take that as a yes."

Rollie drove up highway 99 toward Live Oak, remembering the last time he had been there. He had done a job for a contractor friend, framing up a bay window extension in an old house that was being renovated for some rich rice farmer's son and new daughter-in-law. They had come to the job several times and Rollie had been struck by how young they were and how much money was being spent on them. He had spent several extra hours on the job, not charging for the labor, a sort of present to the young couple that they would never know about, a Doric molding on top of the window that was reminiscent of the Parthenon. An extravagance that would never be noticed, he thought.

He found the address and parked in the street, unsure about how to face this woman whose friend had been wiped out the day before. How do I do this? he asked himself.

"This is your own fault," his wife said. "You could have left the dog with the police and they would have taken care of this."

"I figure I have a responsibility," he said.

"To whom?"

Rollie noticed the grammar. His wife, who had been a teacher all of their married life, had corrected his grammar often enough. She corrected the grammar of newscasters on the television and sometimes the checker at Safeway and their children and, he was sure, St. Peter who had undoubtedly asked her if she was a Presbyterian and he could hear her reply, "If I were a Presbyterian." Which she was.

"To her."

"You don't know her."

"That's not the point. I have the dog, it belonged in the truck, maybe it's a dog she values. Maybe it's all she's got left of him."

"You were never this sensitive when I was around."

"Nonsense, Elaine. Which is one of your favorite words."

"This is nonsense."

Rollie got out of the truck, called to the dog and it came across the seat, dropping to the ground at his feet. As they approached the front door he could see that the dog sensed familiar territory, waiting anxiously at the door, its nose to the screen as Rollie knocked.

The door opened and a woman's face appeared.

"My name is Rollie Decker," he said. "I picked up your dog at the accident yesterday."

She looked down.

"Sweet Jesus," she said, and she opened the screen door, knelt, and embraced the dog, putting her arms around its neck, pulling it toward herself.

Shit, Rollie thought. He was surprised at his reaction. The dog had been with him for less than twenty-four hours, yet he had already grown attached to it, wanted it to sit in the seat of his truck next to him, lie on the porch in the evening as it had done the night before, and it had filled a void in his life that he had not known was there. The woman's face was buried in the dog's shoulder but the dog was looking at Rollie.

When it got hot that afternoon he drove into town to Ray's. It was cool in the bar and dark and he ordered his usual. There were a couple of roofers that he vaguely knew at the bar and he said,

"Too hot to get up on the roof?"

"So damn hot the tar won't set, you walk around in that sticky shit and pretty soon your boots weigh about twenty pounds. Boss said to call it quits."

"You had a call, Rollie," Ray said. He slid a scrap of paper across the bar. "Some guy named MacFerson, said he had a job for you. Said he called your house but nobody answered."

Rollie fingered the paper, took a sip of beer.

"Mind if I use the phone?"

Ray reached under the bar, brought out an old black phone with a dial on the face, set it on the bar. "I am not a goddam answering service, Rollie. This is a bar."

"You took a lot of calls from Elaine."

"That was different, Rollie. All I had to do was say, 'Yes, he was here,' and watch you get up off the stool and head out. I didn't have to write down any messages."

"You're a prince among men, Ray."

"And you're the Bullshit King, Rollie."

It was a job in Live Oak, the same contractor who had hired Rollie to work on the kid's house, and he needed some cabinet work done. I'm supposed to be retired, Harry, Rollie had said, but MacFerson was insistent, Rollie did good work, he was dependable, not like these asshole kids who didn't know which end of the hammer to hold, he was desperate, and it was cash under the table, and Rollie said OK, if it was only a few days. It would be, he knew, a welcome job, something to keep him occupied, out of the rented house in the rice fields, mindless work that would fill a few days.

He had another beer and then Charlie came in and against his better judgment he had another one with Charlie.

"Where's your dog?" Charlie asked.

"The lady who lived with that guy took him back."

"Too bad. He looked like an OK dog." Charlie drained his glass. "You want another one?"

Rollie looked down the bar at Elaine who was shaking her head.

Then he reached into his shirt pocket and took out the folded piece of paper the cop had given him. It had her phone number. He half stood on the bar stool, reached over the bar for the phone.

"Help yourself to the phone, Rollie," Ray said. "Make sure it's a long distance call. Maybe Paris or Calcutta."

"You're still a prince, Ray," Rollie said, dialing the number.

The next morning, on the river road between Live Oak and Hamilton City he waited in the dark. There were headlights that came and went and then a car that slowed, turning into the graveled parking lot. The lights went off and the window went down. And then her voice.

"Rollie. Is that you?"

"Yes."

She got out, went around to the back of the SUV and opened the door. The dog dropped onto the ground, immediately sniffing at Rollie, working out in a wider circle, disappearing in the darkness.

"I wasn't sure you'd come," he said.

"I don't sleep well these days," she said. "I was awake at four." She had a cup of coffee and she sipped from it. He could barely see her outline. She was shorter than he remembered, a slight woman. "I should have brought you a coffee," she said. She held out the cup. "Here."

He took it and sipped, returned it.

"That's OK. I had coffee before I left the house," he lied. "There's a path along the river here. I've fished it before. Steelhead. When the sun comes up over the river it's really something." Rollie looked at the sky beginning to lighten over the distant mountains.

"Can you see OK?" he asked.

"Yes. I'll follow you."

The dog was nowhere to be seen and Rollie whistled. It materialized, was at their side as if he had conjured it with his whistle.

They started along the path and Rollie could feel the river sliding on their left, a steady, powerful surge, a riffle on the far side chuckling but always the insistent rush of water in the gray half light.

He stopped after a few minutes, turned and waited for her to come abreast. It was light enough to see her profile in the false dawn and he wanted to reach out, touch her shoulders, pull her to him.

"Don't be an idiot, Rollie," his wife said. She stood behind the woman, indistinct, but he could hear her voice clearly. Across the river the water was beginning to shine, the surface sliding in the new light, shifting, an almost oily sheen that became purple and then, as the sun rose over the Sierras, the water flamed, and for a moment it was as if the river had caught fire.

"You were right," she broke the silence. "It is something else."

"You want to walk a bit more? I've got time."

"I'd like that," she said. They walked in silence along the river. An egret lifted from the far bank, its wings like white oars rowing rhythmically upstream. The dog came and went, disappearing in the reeds, thrashing about only to emerge on the path ahead of them, pausing to look back, waiting a moment, vanishing again in the underbrush.

Then they turned and came back.

The dog came after them, trotting down to the water's edge while they stood awkwardly beside the vehicles.

"Thanks for coming," Rollie said.

"It was lovely," she replied. "I never knew about this place."

"I've been up and down this river a hundred times," Rollie said. "Probably more. Fishing for steelhead."

"Jimmy liked to hunt."

"I'm not much for that. I used to hunt. Birds. Ducks mostly, sometimes dove. But you have to eat what you shoot and I got so I wasn't keen on that. I can let the steelhead go."

There was another silence and then she called out, "Shoe."

Rollie thought she had said "Shoo!" but when the dog came to her she bent, rubbed its head, said, "Good dog, good Shoe."

"The dog's name is Shoe?"

"Yes."

"Like a shoe on a foot?" Rollie pointed at his boots.

"Yes."

"I've never heard a dog called that."

"The guy who had the litter, he named them. Pants, Shirt, Shoe, Belt, Watch."

"I think I like Watch better than Shoe."

"Jimmy thought it was pretty good. He's part heeler, so Jimmy used to say, If the shoe fits."

She rubbed the dog's head again. "Kind of dumb, isn't it?"

"No. I could get used to it." He immediately regretted what he had said. No, he couldn't get used to it because it wasn't his dog, didn't live with him.

"It's not the name Jimmy called him, though."

"You mean he has two names?"

"Shoe was his puppy name. I still call him that. But Jimmy named him Zack. He had a good friend named Zack when he was a kid . He said Shoe was like Zack, always wanting to please everybody."

I don't want to know any more about Jimmy, Rollie thought. He half expected Jimmy to show up, standing next to his wife, and throw in his two cents worth.

"You want some breakfast?" he asked.

"Rollie," his wife said. "What in the world do you think you're doing?"

If I ignore her, she'll go away. Or at least she'll shut up, Rollie thought. But he knew that wouldn't work.

"Sure," Helena said.

"There's a coffee shop on the main drag that's open at this hour. You know it?"

"The one with the neon sign with the guy flipping a pancake?"

"That's the one."

"I'll follow you," she said.

Rollie's wife was waiting in the truck when he got in.

"Don't say a word," he said. He turned the key .

"Are you trying to get the dog from that woman? Is that what you're trying to do?

"I'm trying to be nice."

"Rollie, I could always see right through you. It was like looking through a window."

"Not always, Elaine. And no, I'm not trying to get the dog away from her."

"She's fragile, Rollie. She lost somebody and here you come, this nice old guy, or at least you're pretending to be this nice old guy and I don't want you to do something you'll regret. Or something that she'll regret."

"What do you think I'm going to do, Elaine?"

"I know you, Rollie Decker. You were about to make a pass at her there on the river."

"If you paid attention, Elaine, you noticed that we took a short walk, watched the sun rise, walked back and now we're going to have ham and eggs in a cafe in the middle of town. You always had a suspicious mind, Elaine." He looked in the rear view mirror and he could see her headlights following.

"You're sixty-five years old, Rollie. You're not some dashing lothario, you know. And she's got to be twenty years younger than you, so don't make a fool of yourself."

"I thought this was about the dog, Elaine."

"It's about you <u>and</u> the dog, Rollie."

"We took a walk, we're going to have breakfast and then I'm going to go make a kitchen cabinet for Harry MacFerson. That's my day, Elaine. And then I'll go home and have a cold beer and sit on the porch of my little rented house and feed the mosquitoes."

"That's another thing, Rollie. Where you live. You need to move out of there. With all those mosquitoes you'll get bitten by one of them that has that vile western virus."

"Western Nile virus, Elaine."

"Well, it's all the same. Anyway, I don't see why you moved out of our perfectly good house in town to live out there."

"Because it was too full of stuff, Elaine. Every time I turned around, I stumbled on something of yours." The cafe was just ahead, and he looked again in the rear view mirror to make sure she had followed.

"They were your things, too, Rollie."

"No, it wasn't my stuff, Elaine. We've had this discussion before. About a hundred times."

"It wasn't stuff, Rollie. There were antiques and fine things. And you sold them to that dealer in town for a song. At least you could have kept some of it. Your daughter might just have wanted that Hepplewhite breakfront."

"I'm sorry, Elaine. I just wanted to clear the decks a bit."

He was in front of the cafe and he turned in to the curb. The SUV pulled in next to his truck .

On the sidewalk he paused, turned to her. "You sure you want to do this?" he asked.

"If I didn't, I wouldn't be here."

She left the dog in the back of her car and inside the cafe they found a booth.

"I can't eat a whole breakfast like this," she said, looking at the menu. "Do you suppose they'd let me order the child's breakfast?"

"Don't see why not."

When the waitress came she asked and was told, "If it's on the menu, you can order it. Makes no difference to me."

The waitress poured coffee and while they waited for their order Helena asked, "What is it you do, Rollie?"

"I've been a carpenter all my life. Built cabinets, houses, you name it. I'm sixty-five, supposed to be retired now, but I still do work for contractors I like, a job here, a job there. That's what I was doing in Grass Valley the other day." He stopped short, not sure if it had been a good idea to remind her of the accident. "Sorry," he added. "I wasn't thinking."

"That's all right," she said. "You don't look sixty-five."

"And you?"

"Me what?"

"What do you do?"

"I'm a school teacher."

"My wife was a school teacher."

"You're married?"

"Not any more. She died two years ago. A stroke. One day she was here and the next day she wasn't"

"Sort of like Jimmy."

"I guess you could say so."

"I'm sorry," she said.

"People always say that. Like it was maybe their fault. I've never understood that."

"I meant I was sorry for your loss."

"I guess I still am married, now that I think about it. I never divorced her. We were married for thirty-eight years. Forty if you count these last two. Although I don't suppose they count, do they?"

She held her coffee cup with both hands, her elbows on the table, looking intently at him.

"What kind of school do you teach?" he asked, steering the talk in another direction.

"Second grade."

They talked easily, their breakfast came, and Rollie realized it was the first time since Elaine had died that he had talked with anyone for a length of time. It felt comfortable and, as the street outside lightened in the morning sun, he wished it could continue.

When she got up to go to the ladies' room Elaine slipped into the booth in her place.

"And just what is this all about, Rollie?"

"It's about having breakfast with a nice woman. Who's interested in me."

"She's being polite, Rollie."

"I can live with that."

"Obviously I can't."

"I'm sorry about the word choice, Elaine. It's not like I poisoned you or threw you off a bridge. You had a stroke."

"And have you brought up the dog yet? That's what this is all about, isn't it?"

"The dog is your issue, Elaine, not mine."

"Nonsense."

Helena came back to the booth and Elaine slid over to make room for her.

"Were you talking to someone?" Helena asked.

"Not really," Rollie said. He looked at Elaine whose mouth was set in a firm line, a sure sign that she had something to say but wasn't about to say it.

She insisted on paying for her breakfast.

"I invited you," Rollie said.

"Doesn't matter," she said, putting a five dollar bill on the table.

Outside, on the sidewalk, she said, "That was nice. The sunrise was spectacular. And Shoe liked the chance to run around." She went to the back of the SUV, opened the lid and took a bottle of water, pouring some in her cupped hand so the dog could lap it up. It slurped noisily as she continued to pour water into her palm.

"Maybe we could do this again," Rollie said.

"Sure. You know where to find me."

But there was something in her voice that told Rollie this was a one-off. Won't happen again, he thought. He reached out to scratch the dog behind the ears.

He worked steadily on MacFerson's cabinet that day, not bothering to stop for lunch, breaking off early and driving back across the valley in the late heat. He stopped at Ray's and had a beer, and then another, and when one of the sheetrockers said he was going down to Jack-in-the-Box to get dinner, Rollie asked him if he'd pick up a Jumbo Jack and some fries.

"It's not going to kill me, Elaine," he said. She had appeared on the bar stool next to him, still silent.

"OK." Rollie turned to face her. "Let's have it. Fire away. Take your best shot, Elaine."

"You never took me to breakfast, Rollie Decker."

"You cooked breakfast every morning."

"I know that. But never once did you say, Elaine, how about going out to breakfast this morning. I know this little place in Live Oak."

"Jesus Christ, Elaine, why would we drive all the way to Live Oak to have breakfast?"

"You drove there this morning. And you went down on the river and showed her the sunrise. You never took me down to the river to show me the sunrise."

"Elaine, she lives in Live Oak. And I had a job in Live Oak today."

"That's not the point, Rollie, and you know it."

Rollie finished his beer. Ray came down the bar and took the glass.

"You OK, Rollie? Sounded like you was arguing with yourself there. Bad day?"

"No, Ray, it was a really good day and the outstanding part is right now, talking to you because you're a real live person, Ray, and I suspect you've got my best interests at heart, especially if I order another beer."

"Don't be a shithead, Rollie."

"It's hard for me to change at this late stage in my life, Ray."

"You want another beer? Maybe you need to go on home, get some shut-eye."

But Rollie didn't go home. He drove back toward Oroville, concentrating hard on the dark road, knowing that if he got stopped by a cop he couldn't pass a sobriety test, but he kept on, hunched over the wheel, fixing himself hard on approaching headlights, the wheel tight in his hands until the other car passed. He drove until he came to the now-closed fruit stand on Highway 20, then turned around, came back along the stretch of road where the accident had been, beginning to sober a bit now, the warm wind whipping in through the open windows. He turned north from Oroville toward Live Oak and when he reached it he drove to her house, passed it, noted the lighted windows, made a U-turn and came back again. He stopped part-way down the block and watched the house for a while, wondering what she was doing, where the dog was and he stayed there until the lights went out.

He drove back through the now darkened town, out to the river road where he found the graveled parking lot next to the river. There was a quarter moon, yellow because of the haze, and he couldn't find a flashlight in the truck. He set out on the path, barely able to make it out in the moonlight. He stumbled along the path, several times nearly falling, catching himself, staggering, and then he stopped, suddenly exhausted. He waited, listening to the river slide in front of him and there was a heavy splash and he knew that the first of the Fall run of salmon was in the river. The noise came again several minutes later, and he knew that a big salmon had rolled in the surface, and that there were others, dark torpedoes that had come two hundred miles from the ocean and would keep on going, some of them up the Yuba, others the Sacramento and these on the Feather ending up at the face of the Big Oro dam, climbing the concrete fish ladders to the hatchery.

And in another month the banks would be littered with the carcasses of spent fish. Come all this way, Rollie thought, lay your eggs and die. But I don't have any eggs. I laid mine years ago and now I'm like those spent fish, drifting down stream, occasionally finning. I'll end up in a backwater, gills opening and closing, turning on my side in the shallows and then I won't be anything any more. He picked his way through the reeds to the edge of the river and lowered himself, sitting on the edge, his legs in the water, boots still on, and he righted himself until he stood calf-deep in the blackness, feeling the tug of the water at his trousers.

"Well, Elaine," he said to the river. "You want to tell me what this is all about?"

There was no answer.

The Boatman

The telephone call came at ten in the morning as Dennis was sweeping the driveway. He almost missed the phone, thought about letting it ring onto the answering machine and then went back into the house to answer. His wife had left to shop for clothes for the grandchildren and Dennis had taken the opportunity to sweep where the car had been parked.

"Dennis?" the voice said.

"Yes."

"You don't recognize the voice?"

It had a familiar ring, and the accent was British and suddenly Dennis knew who it was.

"Terry! I'm sorry, I should have recognized you."

"I'm afraid I've changed a bit, mate. I want to ask you to do something for me."

"Ask away."

"I want you to come to England."

"We were planning on coming in the Fall, Terry. Stop in London, see some theater, then come down to Dorset."

"No, I want you to come now. By yourself."

"What do you mean, now?"

"I mean tomorrow. I'll make all the arrangements, get you a ticket, all you have to do is throw in a change of clothes and get yourself to the airport."

"Good God, Terry, why?"

"Because, old friend, I'm dying. I'm filled with cancer and

I haven't got much time left and I want someone to chauffeur me around for a week and you got the short straw."

"Oh, Jesus, Terry. Why didn't you tell me?"

"I thought I had longer, Dennis. But it's galloping through my brain and suddenly I wanted to go off but I can't drive any more. Christ, I need help to get to the loo."

"Why me?"

"I don't trust any of the people close to me to do what I want them to do. They're all so fucking solicitous. They tell me, yes, Terry, I'll be happy to do that, and then they go off and whisper to each other about how it wouldn't be good for me, as if somehow I can find a miracle cure, but I'm fucking dying, Dennis, and I need some help, and I want you to come."

"Where do you want to go?"

"I'll tell you that when you get here. Will you come?"

Dennis listened to the refrigerator humming and somewhere, outside, a leaf blower whining faintly and then Terry spoke again.

"Dennis, you're retired, you don't have kids at home, it's only a week. We've known each other for thirty years and I trust you. Please."

"Claire has gone shopping. I'll talk it over with her when she gets back, Terry. I'll try to come."

"Don't fucking try! There's nothing to talk over! Tomorrow's Virgin Atlantic flight out of San Francisco. You'll be here Wednesday morning. David will pick you up at Heathrow."

"Why don't you get David to drive you wherever it is you want to go?"

"Because my son loves me and he knows I'm dying and I can't trust him to do what I want. You're a friend, Dennis, not my son. You can do what he can't do."

"This isn't one of those trips to Amsterdam to commit suicide, is it?"

"Oh, Christ, no. It's nothing like that. Please, Dennis, say you'll be here."

It was David who met him at Heathrow, waiting in the knot of people outside the customs gate and David recognized him first. There was only a faint hint of Terry's face in this man and Dennis thought, What happened to you? You were a slim boy with a bicycle who stood, anxious, when I borrowed it to ride down to the pub for more wine during one of those lunches your mother and father threw, and you were waiting to catch me when I wobbled in through the garden gate. And now you're forty years old, stocky, older than we were when we danced on the lawn.

David took his bag.

"How's your father doing?" Dennis asked.

"All right, I suppose. You should be prepared for a change, you know. He's not what you last saw."

"So he told me."

They waited silently at the elevator in the car park and then David said, "Why you? Why didn't he ask me to drive him wherever it is he wants to go?"

"He said you were too close to him. That I would do what you couldn't do. "

"What does he want you to do? Is he going to commit suicide?"

"He laughed when I asked him that. I think his words were, 'Good Christ no!' I have no idea, David. I think he's decided that you love him too much to do whatever it is he wants me to do. Which, by the way, if it's beyond reason, I won't do. You can rest assured of that."

"Do you know where you're going?"

"Not a clue."

David asked no more questions and once they were on the M4, Dennis dozed off, waking when they left the motorway and dropped onto the familiar narrow roads with high hedgerows. It was gray and drizzling by the time they got to the village.

Thirty years ago when they were young and could drink all day and half the night and still go into the classroom the next day and teach, their heads swollen the size of watermelons, thin metal spikes driven through their brains, and they spent all weekend together having lunch, Dennis remembered dancing with Terry on the lawn, children running among the bushes playing hide and seek in the soft English evening. Quite drunk, Terry and Dennis made a pact. If their wives ever grew tired of them, they said, leaning heavily on each other to keep from falling, then they should simply exchange places. That way the children would still have the same people about them and they would all be great friends, only they'd be fucking different partners and when they went into the house to announce this to Claire and Sharon, Claire said, "You two can piss off! First of all, I don't have any desire to shag Terry. He's a nice enough looking man, although he could stand to lose ten pounds and secondly, if you decide to leave me, you can bloody well take the clothes on your back and that's just about all, because I'll take everything else you have and furthermore," Dennis remembered his wife taking a deep breath at this point, " you can both go back outside and consider running off with each other and then you can pass out on the lawn. Sharon and I will do quite well without you two half-wits."

It was quite a performance. It was Sharon who had been hulling the broad beans, and she didn't say anything, and ten years later Terry announced to Sharon that he was leaving her for Nicky, who had been a student of his, had graduated from Cambridge, and had come back to Bryanston to teach history. When they heard about it, Claire said she wasn't surprised. Dennis and Claire continued to see both of them, they seemed to have separated without much rancor, and Sharon married again, an Italian whose sons had gone to Bry and had, coincidentally, been taught by both Terry and Nicky. She moved to Rome and they lost contact with her. But over the years, as Dennis came back to England, Terry became a constant in his life, a familiar touchstone each time he returned.

It had grown dark and Dennis could barely see Terry across the room. He had become insignificant, sunken into the overstuffed chair, and in the gathering darkness he had disappeared until there was only the least shadow of his head and his tired voice. Dennis reached up and pulled the chain on the lamp next to his chair and the yellow light illuminated Terry, who put his hand over his eyes and said, "No, it hurts my eyes now. I'd rather it were dark."

Dennis turned off the lamp and felt for his drink which was, he knew, on the small table next to the chair. He moved his hand carefully so that he wouldn't knock it to the floor, touching the edge of the table, feeling with his fingers until they touched the wet base of the glass. He realized that Terry would, at some point not far off, lose his sight, and he practiced touching the glass, raising it to his lips to sip at the scotch, imagining what it would be like to be blind.

"When I was a lad at Bryanston we had a Greek master who taught mythology," Terry said. His voice came from where the chair was now an indistinct lump against the wall.

"He was supposed to be teaching us the classics, but he got off on all that fucking that went on among the gods and goddesses, and he could read parts of the Iliad in Greek with such intensity you felt you were there, even if you were a dolt who only understood about a fifth of the words. He especially liked the parts where Achilles' captured slave girl was described, her tits and her oiled skin, and we used to think he was positively going to come when Achilles got her back from Agamemnon. It was the same every time."

He stopped talking and Dennis could hear his labored breathing as he struggled to regain his voice. Dennis sipped at the scotch and thought, I'm afraid. I'm afraid that he will die on me some place and I will have to deal with it, and I don't know how.

Terry spoke again.

"But I liked the story of the boatman who ferried people across the Styx. And his dog. I wanted a dog like that. You had a dog, didn't you, Dennis?"

"Yes. Actually my wife had the dog. And the boys. It was a bad-tempered little thing, an ankle biter. A rat-terrier with a mean streak. I grew to like it despite its evil disposition."

"Perhaps Cerberus was a rat-terrier." He stopped again and breathed heavily before resuming.

"You're my boatman, Dennis. You're going to row me across the river."

"Am I supposed to leave you on the other side?"

"You can do as you like, Dennis. I'm half-dead. It's winter. It's a time when we sleep together for warmth only. I want you to hold my hand out to the flame one more time. I want to burn myself. Then you can tip me out of the boat."

"This is fucking nonsense, Terry!"

"Perhaps. Tomorrow we go to York. And from there we go to Hadrian's Wall."

"Why Hadrian's Wall?"

"Have you had moments of passion in your life, Dennis?"

"I'm not sure I understand."

"Moments that imprinted themselves on your brain, moments that keep coming back to you when everything boiled up inside your body, you were filled with love or wonder or absolute hate. But they were moments when you knew you were alive, almost as if you could take one more step and fall off the precipice and fly."

"I suppose so."

"You suppose so! Jesus Fucking Christ, Dennis, let loose before it's too late!"

"You didn't answer my question. Why Hadrian's Wall?"

"Something happened there. To me, not Hadrian. I want to stand in that spot again. And then I want to go find some people and touch them for one last time. One week, Dennis. You row the boat. That's all you have to do."

"And the dog?"

"No dog this time. Just you and me and the ghost of summers past."

Dennis sipped the last of the scotch, carefully set the glass on the almost-invisible table next to his chair.

"I need some sleep, Terry."

"Go on. I'll stay right here. I'll be all right. I often spend nights in this chair. If I need anything, I'll call out."

Dennis rose and went to Terry, bent and touched his shoulder.

"I'm sorry," he said.

"Don't be. That's why I called you. You were the one person I could think of who wouldn't feel sorry for me. All you have to do is row the boat, Dennis."

The wind was blowing hard when he opened the car door. He closed it again and said, "Maybe this isn't such a good idea, Terry."

"You may recall that no one who is close to me thinks you or any part of this trip is a good idea."

"It's a cold wind."

"Blow, winds, and crack your cheeks! rage! blow! You cataracts and hurricanes!" He paused. As if on cue, a spattering of rain swept across the windscreen.

"That's from Lear, Dennis. I did Lear once at Bry. Nicky played the old man. He was brilliant. What cheek I had, casting kids in a play about a dying old man."

The car rocked gently in the wind. Ahead of them a dirt path led up a slope to where it met the wall, a line of closely fitted rocks that rose at the crest, stretching to the right and left with no apparent end.

"Is this the place?" Dennis asked, breaking the silence.

"I think so. It doesn't matter. The wall goes all the way across the country. But it was here that Nicky and I came that first weekend. We stood on the wall and the wind comes up out of the other side, sweeps up a steep slope. It's a braugh Scottish wind, Dennis. We stood there and stretched out our arms like wings and leaned over the edge of the wall, letting the wind hold us up. It was Nicky's idea. I trusted him."

"Do you want to go up to the wall?"

"I'm not sure. It may be enough to just sit here and imagine it."

The rain swept across the windscreen again.

"Besides, we're too old to fly, Dennis. We're two old codgers who would drop like a couple of sacks of potatoes."

"Maybe me. But there isn't enough left of you, Terry. The wind would probably lift you up, spirit you off toward those sheep on the far side of the valley."

"Fair enough," Terry said. "You'll have to put a leash on me, then. Let's do it," and he put his hand on the door handle, turned it, and leaned his shoulder against the door, but he didn't have the strength to make it open.

Dennis came around the car and held open the door for Terry, who grabbed the roof of the car with both hands and hoisted himself to his feet.

"Put rocks in my pockets, Dennis," he said.

"More like rocks in my head," Dennis replied. "For bringing you here."

"Now, now, no whining."

Dennis put his arm around Terry's waist and the two of them went slowly up the path, Dennis lifting Terry slightly with each step. At the edge of the wall the wind came fiercely, and Dennis broke the blast with his body, hoisting Terry up onto the wall. It was wide, grass carpeting the top of it and on the other side it dropped off steeply into the tops of trees and sloping fields beyond.

"It was a day like this," Terry shouted. "Nicky and I stopped on a lark and we climbed up here, or some place just like this, and we opened our jackets and spread them like wings." He began to unzip his jacket and Dennis held him tightly around the waist, afraid that Terry would step to the edge and lose his balance in the stiff wind.

"We spread our arms like this," and Terry stretched out his arms, one in front of Dennis' face, like wings. The jacket flapped in the wind and Dennis could feel the imperceptible lifting of Terry's body.

"And Nicky said, 'come on, lean into it,' and he stood on the edge and leaned over and I thought, Good Christ, he's going to fall, but the wind held him up and I did the same and the two of us hung over the edge like two men gone mad and after we sat in the car and felt each others' bodies and it was like I had been born again."

"You mean it was like a religious experience?"

"Good Christ, no! No fucking way. It was an experience of passion, joy so complete that I thought the rest of my life would be downhill. And, in some ways it was."

He half-turned toward the car. "Time to go, Dennis. I'm freezing my arse off."

They came off the motorway among factories, industrial buildings, blackened brick, onto streets crowded with lorries and cars, and Terry woke. Dennis, aware again that he was driving on the wrong side of the road, concentrated, approaching a roundabout when suddenly Terry said, "It's as if I never left this place. I haven't been here in thirty years, yet I know where I am."

It took half an hour of working through the traffic until they came into a neighborhood of narrow streets, Victorian row houses, identical grimy brick buildings, the only difference being the painted door on each one.

"Go slow," Terry said. "It's in the next block."

Rubbish bins lined the curb and water glistened with an oily sheen in puddles along the curbing. It was not a good neighborhood, and the windows were sometimes sheeted with a piece of wood, others had trash piled in the lee of the stone stairways that led to each front door.

"There," Terry said. "The one with the red door." He pointed to one of the flats fronted by a door painted fire-engine red.

"The old bugger still does it," he said. "Every year, like clockwork, he painted that door, made me scrape the old paint off, right down to the bare wood. 'Do it right, lad, or don't do it at all,' but of course I didn't have the option of not doing it at all. He'd inspect it and if there was a single speck of old paint left I had to go at it again. I wanted to be out here in the street with my mates kicking a football, but no, the old bastard wanted that door as smooth as a baby's bum, and then he'd put on three coats, rub each one, you'd think it was a Rolls Royce. Park there."

He pointed to a space just in front of the flat and Dennis pulled up next to the curb.

"All right," Terry said, "Steel yourself. You're about to meet the troll who lives under the bridge."

He didn't move, breathing heavily, and then he said, "You'll have to go up to the door, Dennis. Tell him I'm here. He may not let me in."

Dennis got out of the car, climbed the steps and raised the knocker on the door. It was an ornate brass knocker, polished until it shone, and it wasn't the usual lion with a ring in its mouth or a gargoyle. It was the face of a man, bald-headed, not one of those Greek or Roman faces, but a modern man with the knocker ring through his nose, the nostrils raised to accommodate it.

He waited, knocked again and the door opened. The man facing him was short, stocky, dressed in blue work pants and a blue work shirt with a wide leather belt and a round pot belly that hung over it. But he didn't look fat, just beefy like a fireplug with white hair that flew from his head, sprouted from his ears and nostrils. His face was wizened and Dennis was startled to see Terry's features but it was as if someone had carved Terry onto an apple and the apple had dried, like an apple-faced doll, the cheeks folded, the chin sunken into this tiny old man's face.

"What do you want?" he said.

"I'm a friend of your son, Terry,"

"I don't have a son," he said.

"You're Mr. Ellis?"

"That's right."

Dennis turned toward the car at the curb. ""Your son, Terry is here. He'd like to see you."

The old man squinted at the car, then at Dennis. "He's no son of mine," he said. "Not unless he's changed."

"He's changed, Mr. Ellis," Dennis said. Ellis squinted again at the car, trying to see more of Terry, who was slumped against the window. Not the way you think, you old asshole, Dennis thought.

"He's not feeling well. I'll help him up," and Dennis went back down the steps to the car, knocked on the window. Terry moved his head, looking at him through the fogged glass.

Dennis opened the door.

"Am I the prodigal son?" Terry asked.

"Not quite."

"Bugger all," Terry said. "This may be a huge mistake, Dennis. If it is, will you forgive me? You won't abandon me here, will you?"

"That remains to be seen," Dennis, said, sliding his hand under Terry's armpit, helping him to his feet on the sidewalk. As they turned, Dennis could see the old man inside the half-opened door He was watching the two of them carefully.

You probably think I'm his queer mate, you old prick, Dennis thought. Go ahead, think away. They slowly ascended the stairs and Dennis pushed the door open, and Terry, suddenly mustering some reserve of energy, was on his own, walking into the little hallway.

"Hello, Da," he said. "How've you been?"

His father said nothing, watching as Terry entered the parlor, steadied himself on the back of an overstuffed chair, and slowly lowered himself, careful, Dennis noted, not to show any pain or discomfort. It was a small room, fronted onto the street with a tiny bay, the backs of the chairs covered with doilies, heavy lace curtains muting the view, an ugly Wilton carpet of rose and intertwined flowers dominating everything. Mr. Ellis sat in a chair opposite Terry.

"Your friend here says you've changed. What does that mean?"

"It means I'm sick, Da. I'm dying and I wanted to come and see you and I'm hoping you'll at least talk to me." His voice had risen an octave, and it was beginning to sound like the voice of a boy asking his father for permission to stay out late and Dennis thought, Oh shit, this was a bad idea, Terry.

The old man looked at Terry silently for what seemed like a minute and then he spoke.

"So, you're still a poufter are you? And this," he pointed to Dennis, "is your queer mate, is he?"

"No, Da. Dennis is an old friend and he's got a wife and two kids and no, he's not queer."

"But you are."

"You know that, Da."

"Then you're no son of mine."

"How old are you now, Da?"

"What's that got to do with anything?"

"What is it, ninety-three? Ninety-four? Christ, Da, you're older than Methuselah. Surely you've seen worse things in your life than me."

"No son of mine is bent." He put his hands on the arms of the chair, heaved himself erect and turned to walk from the room.

"Da!" Terry called out, and Dennis thought, now, this is the time, right now. Get up and walk from this house and drive off some place and have a drink and forget this ugly scene in this ugly one-act play.

Terry's father stopped. Without turning, he said, "When you played rugby at school, you gave no quarter. You was a right proper rugger, you was. You come home bloodied and I was proud of you."

"I wasn't that keen about rugby, Da. I did that for you."

The old man turned to face Terry. "You was good at it. Fearless, you was. How could you do that and turn into what you are?"

"I didn't turn into anything, Da."

"Yes, you did! You had a wife and a boy."

"I still have David. I'm still his father. Same as you're still my father."

The old man shifted his gaze to Dennis.

"What's he dying of?"

"Ask him."

"I'm asking you."

"And it's not my place to answer that question. You can't bully me, Mr. Ellis. I'm not afraid of you."

Ellis snorted.

"I'm not afraid of him, Dennis," Terry said. "There was a time when I was afraid. Just the sound of him coming up the steps and opening the door was enough to send me scurrying. But not any more." He turned toward his father. "Not any more, Da. I don't need your approval. I'm filled with cancer. It's not AIDS, which, I suspect, you think it is, and it didn't come because I'm bent, it just came to me and flowered inside my body."

Terry paused, sucked in his breath before continuing.

"I don't know what I expected would happen when I came here today. But I had to come. See you one more time. And now that's done," he said, grasping the arms of the chair and, with some effort, rising.

"You're going?" Ellis said.

"I think we've said everything,"

"You asked how old I am. It's a terrible thing to outlive all your family and all your mates. There's nobody left who knows who I am."

"You have a grandson."

"Yes."

Terry stood, gathering himself. "Well, then, Da," he said, "It's goodbye."

"Yes."

Jesus Christ, Dennis thought, you can't just end it this way, but Terry was moving toward the door and the old man remained rooted in place, unwavering. The old son of a bitch won't give an inch, Dennis thought. He's hurting and he's watching his only son climb into his coffin and he stands there like some fucking spectator watching a stranger leave the room. Jesus, Terry, you can't drive all the way here and say ten words to each other and walk away. But Terry was in the hallway, turning toward Dennis.

"Dennis?"

They went down the steps in silence, Terry leaning heavily on Dennis' arm. He opened the passenger door, watched while Terry gripped the edge of the car roof and lowered himself into the seat. As he came around the car, Dennis looked up at the house. The curtain was held back just enough to reveal the old man watching. Then he let go of the curtain and was no longer visible.

Dennis closed the car door, inserted the ignition key, turning toward Terry.

"Christ, Terry, I don't fucking believe what just happened."

"He's a piece of work, my old man, isn't he?"

"What was the point?"

"Of what?"

"Of coming here?"

"It was something I had to do."

"What did you do? We weren't there half an hour. I don't think there were fifty words spoken."

"My old man was never one for talking. I used to wonder how my mother could stand the silence. Like Siberia it was."

"You weren't exactly talkative in there."

"We both said what we had to say. I wanted him to see me one last time. Remind him that David is his grandson. He's like the dodo bird, is my old man.. Only everything around him is going extinct and he's still alive. He's too fucking pig-headed to die. Stands there and he says to God, 'I'll not go until I say so, so bugger off. And take those fairy angel wings with you!'"

Terry was smiling now.

"Come on, Dennis, row the fucking boat. We're starting to drift downstream."

"Where to?" Dennis asked.

It was gray and threatening rain again and the traffic on the ring road was mostly lorries, filling both lanes, going too fast, Dennis felt. He hoped that they would leave the motorway soon.

"Gatwick," Terry said.

"Gatwick? The airport?"

"Yes."

"Are we meeting someone?"

"No, we're going some place."

"Jesus Christ, Terry, you said I was going to drive you. You never said we were flying some place."

"It's not far."

"Where?"

"To Rome. To see Sharon. She's expecting us."

"And you expect to get on an airplane and fly to Rome and fly back just like that? You could barely climb the steps to your father's house."

"It's mostly sitting, Dennis. You can wrap me in a raincoat and help me on the plane and I'll sit in my seat and take my drugs and you can drink a double scotch and before you know it, we'll be in Rome."

Dennis felt his hands tightening on the steering wheel.

"You've got this all planned, haven't you? What else is there that you haven't told me?"

"Nothing. The rest is straightforward. We'll be in Rome for a night. We'll come back the next day. I'll be all right, I promise you."

"Why didn't you tell me this before we left Dorset?"

"Because I was afraid you wouldn't do it. I want to see Sharon one more time, Dennis. Remember when I asked you if you had moments of passion in your life?"

"Yes."

"Well, Sharon was one of those moments. Together we have a son. He's a bit of a stodgy lad. Shit, he's no lad any more. He's a grown man. But he loves me and I love him and without Sharon he would never have existed. I want to touch her one more time, Dennis. Thank her. You were there, Dennis. We danced in the garden, drank wine until the stars came out. Oh Christ, this is getting maudlin. I want to go out like Gully Jimson, painting my way down the Thames. Go with me to Rome, Dennis. I can't do it by myself."

"One night?"

"That's all."

"You promise you won't die in Rome?"

"I'm an Englishman, Dennis. It's against the rules."

"Bullshit. France is full of dead Englishmen. So is Italy. And North Africa and India. There are more dead Englishmen outside England than inside. You've got bodies scattered all over the world."

"They got shot, Dennis. It doesn't count. Nobody is going to shoot me in Rome."

"I might."

"Wait until the end of the week, will you?"

There was an orange glow in the sky as the plane descended into Rome, the ground obscured in a soft haze, the darkness growing as they descended. Terry was awake now, and when the plane stopped the cabin erupted in a flurry of passengers rising, pulling down bags from the overhead compartments, standing in the aisle, shoulder to shoulder, waiting for the door to open. Dennis waited for the plane to clear and when he saw a flight attendant coming back down the empty aisle he rose, pulled their bag from the open rack and reached down to undo Terry's seat belt. Terry pulled himself erect, using the back of the seat to steady himself.

"Do you need assistance?" the young man asked, now at Dennis' side.

"No, I think we can manage," Dennis said, and he steadied Terry, who worked his way toward the front of the craft, holding each seat back as he passed.

Dennis turned to the attendant, now following them up the aisle and said, " A wheelchair would help."

"Good Christ, I'm not a fucking cripple," Terry said, but he said it without emphasis, and Dennis knew that he wouldn't object to being wheeled through the Rome airport.

A raw wind swirled around the taxi stand outside the terminal where Terry spoke to the driver leaning against the taxi, explaining in fluent Italian where they wanted to

46

go. "Per favore mi porti a questo indirizzo," he said, adding, "it's close to piazza Navonna."

They whipped through the narrow streets, weaving in and out of traffic and Terry smiled as the driver said something in Italian, waving his hand at a car in front of them, suddenly slipping between the stopped car and the wall of a building with only inches to spare, gesturing again at the driver, a man who waved his hand back, mouthing words at the taxi driver.

"I love them," Terry said. "Nobody gets really angry, but they swear at each other, call each other idiots and cretins, drive like maniacs. There's so much energy here."

"It scares the shit out of me," Dennis said.

"It's the Germans who frighten me," Terry said. "They're humorless and they drive at insane speeds on the autobahn, but of course we Brits aren't much better." He leaned forward, said, "Per favore, guidi piu adagio." Then he added, "You can kill me, but leave my friend alive, d'accordo?"

The taxi driver turned around, smiling, and said, "It's a new Mercedes. Nobody dies in one of these."

The hotel was small, only seven rooms, narrow windows with shutters onto the cobbled alley. Dennis went out to find a coffee while Terry rested and by the time Dennis came back Sharon was there. She looked as he imagined she would look, a handsome woman in her early sixties, no longer the slender mum in a hippie blouse with skirt dragging at her bare feet. Now she wore a tailored suit and her hair was cut short and she greeted Dennis effusively, hugging him, whispering in his ear as she did so, "Good God, he looks a wreck."

"You two want me to go for a walk?" Terry asked.

"And why would we want that?" Sharon asked.

"It appears you fancy my driver, Sharon. He is a handsome beast, isn't he?"

They talked about children and Claire and old times and Terry told her that they had been to see his father.

"And?" she said.

"No different. He liked you, Sharon. He liked the idea of you and me."

"It was a bit more than an idea, you twit."

Dennis was reminded of Claire calling the two of them twits one Sunday afternoon when they'd had too much to drink and he could see Sharon at the kitchen sink, hulling beans, and he wished that somehow he could turn the clock back, but there was, of course, no point in thinking that, and he watched her talking with Terry, listened to the lilt in her voice, something different about it now, and Dennis realized that her English accent was tinged with Italian. Where was the Italian husband, he wondered.

They talked while the room darkened and then it began to rain and Dennis found a trattoria and brought back pasta and bread and wine and they ate in the room and Terry fell asleep.

"He's in terrible condition, isn't he?" Sharon said.

"Yes. He'll wake later and he'll be in pain and I'll help him with the morphine and take him to the loo. It's all very undignified. We're back to basics, I'm afraid."

"Terry was never very dignified. I can't remember how many times they would have sacked him at Bry if he hadn't been able to get brilliant performances out of those boys. He liked being the court jester."

"You two were good together."

"We were the best of friends. But we were never lovers. Oh, we slept together and we had David but when he told me about Nicky, it was a kind of relief. But I do love him. He's one of a kind, Dennis."

They put on their coats and went down to the street and walked until they came to a church and Sharon said, "I want to light a candle for Terry."

They went into the dark church. The sexton had come to the door and said something and Sharon replied in Italian.

."He says he's locking up, but he'll wait a few moments for us," and she went to an altar in a niche along the wall of the nave and lit a candle, kneeling to offer a prayer. Dennis was sure that she had not been a Catholic when he had known her in England. He watched her and then dropped the coins in his pocket in the wooden box and lit a candle, but he didn't kneel to pray.

Back at the hotel, Terry was still sleeping and they took the rest of the bottle of wine to Dennis' room and finished it and then Sharon said, "It's time for me to go."

"It's raining. It's late. You can stay here."

"Probably not a good idea, Dennis."

"No, it's late, you've had some wine, the roads will be wet and you said it's more than an hour's drive. I'll be the gentleman. You can keep your knickers on."

"And what would Claire say to that?"

"I wouldn't tell her. Nor will you."

So Sharon stayed, and Dennis sat at one of the windows listening to the whine of Vespas and the voices of people below in the street while Sharon went into the tiny bathroom and then Sharon slipped into the bed and he turned out the light and got into the bed next to her, careful not to touch her.

"Good night," he said.

"It appears," she said, "that I've parked in a No Fucking zone."

"And if we violate the ordinance, is there a fine?"

"Probably the rest of your life in jail."

Dennis reached over and touched her hair, ran his fingers along her jaw, touching her lips.

"Good night," he said.

He awoke to the sound of birds. It was dark in the room, the shutters closed, and when Dennis put his feet on the terrazzo floor it was cold. He opened the shutters and there was rain still pattering on the cobblestones below. Somewhere overhead were geese and he listened to their honking until it faded. He could hear her breathing behind him and he closed the shutters again and listened in the darkness to the steady susuration of her breath and it comforted him. He went into the bathroom, turned on the light and looked at his watch. It was two o'clock. It would be four o'clock in the afternoon at home. He looked at himself in the mirror, thought, this year I will be sixty-eight years old. How did I get to be this old? It was as if he had no past, only this present moment in a foreign country with the rain falling gently, and he thought of that afternoon in the church, watching her light a candle for Terry, lighting a candle himself, telling her that he was lighting it for Terry, too, but knowing that he was lighting it for her, hoping that she had found happiness and something that would calm the panic that, somehow, he knew bubbled up inside her from time to time. He had forgotten how to pray. She did it easily, kneeling at the altar, crossing herself and he had watched the back of her head, her hair caught inside the collar of her coat. The church had been cold and dim, with candles in altars flickering in the far corners. He had, at that moment, found himself filled with so much love for her that he thought he would burst. And now, the cries of the geese came again as they circled in the night, and he felt her presence and, feeling his way to the bed he slipped in beside her. She radiated warmth and the shuddering of his body slowed and in her sleep she put her arm across him and he felt complete.

It was a tiny glass heart made of Murano glass and he wished he had bought it the previous day. Now the shop was closed. It was a tiny shop facing a narrow walk, rain dimpling the surface of the puddles where the light from the shop window illuminated the water. The glass heart glowed as if it were infused with blood, the rich oxygenated blood that flows from the heart. The price tag was only ten euros, about ten dollars, but he knew that the shop wouldn't open until long after they had left for the airport. He had, the afternoon before when he had gone out for coffee, bought a tiny glass penguin, not much more than a quarter of an inch tall, pure white and rich black with orange flippers and a beak of orange glass that was drawn out into a needle point. He could not imagine someone being able to make something so small and delicate. As a child he had a glass animal collection, and great aunts and his mother and his aunt had, on special occasions, bought him a glass animal and they all lay in a wooden box in a drawer now, nestled in cotton. He hadn't added anything to the collection since he was a child. He wished the shop were open so that he could buy the heart for Claire. Perhaps she would have placed it on the table next to their bed, or put it on a shelf in the living room where guests would have fingered it and asked, "where did this come from?"

"Rome," she would have said. "It was a gift."

Back in the hotel Terry was awake, and Dennis set the two cups of coffee on the table next to the bed.

"Something to get your heart started," he said.

Terry sipped at the coffee and made a face. "Needs hemlock," he said.

There was a knock at the door and when Dennis opened it, the desk clerk was there.

"Your taxi, signore. It is here."

Dennis took a last swig of coffee and wrapped a coat around Terry, putting his arm around him and helping him to his feet. He motioned to the bag and the clerk took it.

As they got out of the taxi at the airport, Terry said, "I'm not sure I can make this."

"What do you mean?"

"I feel shitty."

"That's nothing new."

"I mean it, Dennis. I'm not sure I can do this."

"Goddamit, you'll do it. I don't know enough Italian to do more than find the men's toilet and I want to get you back to England so you'll goddam well do it!"

"Your solicitude is touching."

"Just let me row the goddam boat, Terry."

Once they were on the plane, Terry sank into his seat and said to Dennis, "Drugs. Knock me out, mate."

Dennis fished in the carry-on, found the morphine tablets and within a few minutes Terry's eyes glazed over.

A half hour into the flight Terry mumbled to Dennis that he needed to go to the loo and Dennis helped him to his feet, helped him down the aisle, helped him into the tiny toilet and waited outside. The stewardess watched him carefully. Another passenger lined up, and then another and Dennis grew anxious. There were three of the little toilets, but Terry had been in one of them for too long, and Dennis knocked on the door, put his face to it and said, "Terry? All right in there?"

There was no answer and panic swept over Dennis. The other passengers and the stewardess were too close, and the stewardess said, "Is your friend sick? "

"Yes. Is there a way to open this door from the outside?"

But before she could answer, Dennis heard Terry's voice, indistinct, and the lock on the door snapped. Dennis opened the door a crack and saw that Terry's body was on the floor, and there was the smell of shit and he opened the door wide enough to go in, hearing the stewardess' voice saying, "Sir, there can't be two of you in there!" but he had the door closed and locked and in the space barely large enough for himself and Terry he saw that Terry was crumpled over the toilet and there was shit all over his legs and his trousers and Terry was crying, saying, "Christ, Dennis, I've shat myself. I can't control myself any more."

"We'll clean you up. Don't worry. I'll make it OK"

"You can't fucking make it OK, Dennis. I'm sorry. I'm so sorry."

Dennis hoisted Terry around until he was sitting on the toilet, pulled off his trousers and washed them in the little basin. He stripped off paper towels, wet them, and managed to clean Terry's legs. He washed out the shorts, wrung them as dry as he could, and put them back on, stuffing them with clean paper towels.

There was a knock on the door and the voice of a man saying, "This is the flight engineer. You need to come out of there."

"Back off!" Dennis shouted. "Give me five minutes and I'll have him out. Just back off, will you?"

There was silence from the other side of the door.

"I was never one for meeting men in toilets, Dennis. I hope you know that."

Dennis smiled.

"I stink, don't I?" Terry said. "How can I go back out there?"

"We'll go back out there and sit in our seats and I'll make farting noises and keep apologizing in a loud voice and they'll all blame it on the uncouth American. Are you all right now?"

"No. I feel like shit. Sorry about that. Bad choice of words."

"But you can make it back to your seat?"

"I'll need help."

"I'll help you."

"I've asked you to do more than row the boat, haven't I?"

"Just shut up and lean on me."

Dennis opened the door and found himself facing a knot of passengers, a man in a pilot's uniform, and the stewardess. "Give us room," he said.

They moved back against the bulkhead and Dennis pulled Terry from the toilet, putting his arm under Terry's arm, and they started back up the aisle.

"Sir?" It was the uniformed man.

"Not now," Dennis said. "After we get to our seats, OK?"

He walked Terry up the aisle, the heads of passengers swiveling to follow their progress and when he had eased Terry into his seat, and buckled the seat belt, he covered Terry with a blanket, then turned to face the uniformed man who had followed him.

"What's your friend's problem?"

"He's sick."

"I can see that."

"Actually, he's dying, but he's promised not to die on your aircraft, so if you'll leave us alone and make sure there's a wheelchair waiting when we land, I promise you there won't be any more trouble."

"I need to know more specifically what his condition is."

"All you need to know is that he's sick and he's embarrassed by all of this and it will be best if you go back to the cockpit and let me take care of him for the rest of the flight. We must have less than an hour in the air and then you'll be rid of us forever."

Dennis eased himself back into his seat, and, looking up at the uniformed man, thought, Christ, I'm in charge here. He's afraid of me and afraid of Terry, afraid that Terry will die on his airplane, but I'm not afraid.

Dennis buckled his seat belt and the man said, "If there's any problem, the stewardess will let me know."

"I'm sure she will. She's very efficient."

Dennis reached down into the carry-on, took out the bottle of morphine tablets and shook two into his palm. He dropped the bottle back into the bag and took Terry's face in one hand, pressing the pills into his mouth. He took the bottle of water from the seat pocket and tipped it carefully. Terry swallowed, his eyes closed. Dennis knew that the uniformed man was watching him intently.

"Everything's all right, now," Dennis said. Terry nodded.

Dennis watched the back of the uniform go up the aisle, then reached over and pressed the button to recline Terry's seat.

"You all right?" Dennis asked.

"Captain Courageous, that's you," Terry whispered. "God, what a performance. Can you fly the fucking airplane, too?"

"Probably."

They waited until the plane emptied before Dennis took the blanket from around Terry and helped him undo his seat belt. He looked up to see two paramedics coming down the aisle, followed by the man in the pilot's uniform.

"It's all right," Dennis said. "We can make it on our own."

"Just wait a moment, sir," the first one said. "If you don't mind, we'd like to check the gentleman first." He set a first aid box on the seat in front of them, opened it and took out a stethoscope. Reaching past Dennis, he took Terry's wrist, held it, and watched his wristwatch as he counted the pulse.

"What seems to be the gentleman's problem?"

"He's got cancer and he's dying and we'd like to get home."

"Is he in much pain right now?"

Dennis looked at Terry, who nodded.

"Yes," said Dennis

"Is someone meeting you?" the paramedic asked Dennis, leaning in to place the stethoscope against Terry's chest.

"Hello," Terry said. "You can talk to me. I'm not dead yet."

"Sorry," the paramedic said, straightening up. "Are you on medications?"

"Heroin." Terry said. "Meths. Morphine. Bovril. Newcastle Brown."

"He hasn't lost his sense of humor, has he," the medic said to Dennis.

"There you go again, talking to him. Just because he's better looking and hasn't soiled his pants you're chatting him up. You ought to be ashamed of yourself."

"I think," the medic said, turning to the man in the uniform, "that Mr. Ellis can make it out to the gangway with a little help." He turned back to Dennis.

"You have someone meeting you?"

"No. We've got a car. If you could go out to the car park with us and watch Mr. Smarty-pants here while I bring it around, it would be a big help."

"More like Mr. Shitty-pants, Dennis."

It was amazing, Dennis thought, as he brought the car down the ramp toward the two paramedics who were waiting with Terry in a wheelchair. He came alive with those two, even though he had to be in pain and his trousers were wet and he smelled like shit and he looked like shit, but somehow he had glued himself together and he had charmed them.

The two paramedics lifted Terry into the back seat, wishing him good luck. Dennis noticed that they both called him Terry. As they left the airport, Terry said, "In to London, Dennis."

"No, we're going down to Dorset. Get you home and into bed."

"One last stop. I want to see Nicky."

"For Christ's sake, Terry, you're in no condition to see anyone."

"We can stop at Marks and Sparks and you can buy me some clean clothes. We'll get a hotel room and I can clean up, shower off, and we'll go see Nicky and then we'll go back home. I promise, Dennis."

They took a taxi across the Waterloo Bridge to the National. There was a steady stream of people crossing the concrete arcade along the Thames toward the theater. A sharp wind came off the river and it was a relief to get inside the crowded lobby. Dennis asked Terry if he wanted a drink, and Terry laughed. "Christ, I can barely stand now," he said.

They had seats in the last row of the stalls, on the aisle, at Terry's' insistence.

"I doubt if I'll last the first act," he said.

Nicky had telephoned the box office, reserved tickets for them and at the last minute, as the house lights dimmed, Dennis helped Terry to his seat.

Nicky was Richard II, striding onto the stage as the lights went up, and he filled the theater with his presence, larger than life, a middle-aged man who was nothing like the willowy young man Dennis remembered and Dennis was lost in the play when he felt Terry's tug at his arm.

"Now," Terry hissed in his ear and they rose in the dark, Dennis holding Terry up, leading him to the door, out into the bright foyer. Terry's face was ashen and Dennis held him up, an arm around Terry's waist. Outside, Dennis hailed a taxi but no sooner had they crossed the bridge than Terry said, "I need to find a loo. Now."

The taxi stopped in front of a pub and Dennis helped Terry out, handing the driver a fiver, too much since they had only been in the taxi a few hundred yards. Inside the pub they found the men's toilet and Dennis helped Terry off with his raincoat, unbuckled his trousers and steadied him on the toilet. Then he waited, leaning against the wall of the stall, both of them silent, until Terry said, "I can manage now," and Dennis left the stall, waiting for Terry outside, washing his hands deliberately in the grungy sink.

Upstairs in the pub they took seats near the open door, looking out into the gray street. Rain began to dimple the puddles on the pavement and across the street on the side of a red London double-decker was an advertisement that ran the length of the bus, a photograph of a young couple standing in blue water, a white beach behind them and the words "Why not go where the sun shines?" Dennis remembered standing in water like that in Mexico once, but it seemed as if it had happened to someone else in another life.

He ordered half pints, sat nursing his while Terry's glass was ignored. He seems to grow smaller, Dennis thought, the raincoat bunching over Terry's shoulders, his hands almost lost in the sleeves.

"You all right?" Dennis asked, leaning closer to Terry.

"At this moment. Isn't he brilliant?"

"Nicky?"

"Who else. I wish I could have stayed. Oh God, Dennis, there are lines in the second act that sing. 'Let's talk of graves, of worms, and epitaphs, make dust our paper, and with rainy eyes write sorrow on the bosom of the earth. And nothing can we call our own but death.'"

Terry smiled, then said, "I can still remember things, Dennis. There's a bolt of lightning that goes through my brain once a minute, but I can still remember the fucking lines."

He reached out and gave his glass a quarter turn. He spoke again, this time not looking at Dennis, his eyes fixed on the open door.

"We had a boy at Bry whose name was Josef. He was a black boy from the Congo. Father was some sort of diplomat. Josef had a face that shone like ebony. We were making sets for The Tempest and Josef stepped on a nail, came hobbling to me with a piece of wood stuck to his foot. I had him sit down and I took his foot in my hand and when I started to pull the nail out—it wasn't a big nail, nothing serious—he said, 'If I were nkisi you could die.'

"I didn't understand. What I thought he said was 'If I were in Keesee, you could die,' and I thought it was a place in the Congo. I said, 'Is that where you live?'"

Terry's voice had steadied, as if the remembrance of a long-past event had brought with it something of his own past strength.

"'No,' Josef said, 'Nkisi is a little wooden man. You stick nails in him to remember a grandfather when he dies or if you have an enemy you can accuse him of something and spit on the nail when you drive it in. My father told me there was once an nkisi in every village and a man in the village who knew the story behind every nail. And if a man said he was falsely accused, he could pull out the nail, but if he was guilty, he would die.' Then Josef said, 'Pull it, Sir,' and I pulled out the nail and painted his heel with anti-septic and he laughed and said I obviously wasn't guilty."

"What's this story got to do with us, Terry? Is there a point to it?"

"The point is, I'm pulling nails out, Dennis. And I'm going to die."

"Does that mean you're guilty of something?"

"We're all guilty of something, Dennis. The little wooden man must look like a hedgehog with my nails. You, too, mate. You've got a few nails in there."

"Nothing worth dying over."

"You expect me to believe that?"

"No."

"I thought not. Christ, Dennis, you're a secretive man. You're a fucking time bomb, aren't you?"

"What if I don't feel guilty, Terry? What if I decide that everything I've ever done is just that, nothing more, nothing less, just things that happened and I'm not guilty of anything. At least I don't think so. Your father thinks you're guilty. But you don't, do you?"

Dennis waited for an answer, leaning forward across the scarred pub table, suddenly aware of the smell of wet wool and cigarettes and stale beer and the rush of the traffic beyond the door and the metallic aftertaste of the beer in his mouth, as if his senses had been sharpened. Someone had turned up the volume inside his brain.

David was waiting when they arrived and he helped Terry into the house while Dennis followed with the bag. Terry sank into the overstuffed chair and remained motionless, staring straight ahead. When he spoke, it was with difficulty and they both strained to hear him

"Tablets," he said. He waited while Dennis got the bottle out of the bag.

"Three enough?"

"No, more than that."

"We need to be careful."

"Why?"

David was there with a glass of water and held it to his father's lips. Terry sank back, closing his eyes.

"He's much worse," David said.

"Yes. It took a lot out of him."

"Where did you go?"

"We went to Hadrian's Wall and we saw your grandfather and your mother and Nicky."

"Mother's in Rome!"

"Yes. That part wasn't easy. In fact, none of it was easy."

Faint words came from Terry: "I'm not dead, yet."

"You give a good imitation," Dennis said.

"Give me another week," Terry said. "I'll have it polished up. I'll look so fucking dead you'll have me carted off in a pine box."

"Don't talk that way, Dad," David said.

Dennis and David went into the kitchen where there was coffee on the stove and a plate with cheese and bread.

"I thought you might be hungry," David said.

"What I really need is a scotch over ice," Dennis said. "A big one."

He and David sat at the kitchen table and Dennis told David about the trip, skipping the scene on the airplane, assuring him that his father and his grandfather had talked with each other, that there seemed to be an air of forgiveness. He passed along Sharon's greetings and told him about seeing Nicky's performance. All of it was sugar-coated and he wondered at the ease with which he lied.

It wasn't that he wasn't telling David the truth, but he was re-inventing the trip, taking out pieces, sewing it together in a form that would, he knew, be an easier one for David to hear. And as he talked, he listened to himself and he thought, sometimes I no longer know what is true and what I have invented. I say something and it becomes the truth. I am standing in a trattoria in Rome and the old waiter gestures in Italian while I try vainly to tell him that I want to take some pasta with me and I need a bottle of wine. He points to a shelf and suddenly he is pointing to a bottle of ice wine and I am imagining the ice wine in a slender glass, and Claire is sitting opposite me in a restaurant, we have finished dinner, and there is this delicate amber cast to the wine, the surface of the glass touched with frost, and I lean forward and I am there and it really happened. It's as if the ice wine is there, in the glasses in our hands, and it is the truth, so that when you ask, "was there really a glass of ice wine?" I answer, "yes," and part of me knows that it is a lie and some other part of me says, no, it's the truth. There really was a glass of wine. Perhaps Claire wasn't there. Perhaps that part is a lie. But the wine was there in that frosted glass and it tasted cold and sweet and she would have loved it, too.

He realized that he had stopped talking and David was looking closely at his face.

"Do you see your mother often?" Dennis asked.

David paused, as if listening for his father in the other room, and then said, "No. She comes a few times a year to see her grandchildren. When she and Dad split up I was boarding at Bry and then she met Stefano and moved to Rome and when I was finished at Bry I went off to University. I spent more time with Dad than with her. Sometimes a holiday in Rome. Mostly when I was at Cambridge, I came down here on holiday with Dad and Nicky. Nicky was like an older brother in a lot of ways. He's only seven years older."

Dennis was conscious of the humming of the refrigerator and he thought of the afternoon Terry had called, the humming of the refrigerator in his own kitchen. And here was David, in his forties, his children the same age he had been when Dennis and Terry had danced on the lawn. He wondered if David remembered waiting for him to come back from the pub, drunk, riding David's bike.

"Will you be all right here, tonight?" David asked.

"Yes."

"I'll come back tomorrow morning. I'm taking time off from work to watch him."

"That's good."

"Hospice will take him next week."

"Does he know that?"

"Yes."

"Do you remember, when you were a boy, I borrowed your bicycle one Sunday and rode off to the pub for more wine? I was really drunk and you waited at the gate for me."

"Yes. You were so pissed I had to catch you when you came in the gate."

"You were only ten."

"I have a son who is ten."

"And do you get pissed and borrow his bicycle and ride off to the pub?"

David laughed. "Some things you can't do over again. You and Dad were two of a kind."

After David had gone Dennis helped Terry to the loo, stood there holding his shoulders while he emptied his bowels, then helped him out of his clothes, sponged him off and put a dressing gown around him. Once back in his chair, Terry said, "You've been a good mate, Dennis. You've done more than I would have asked."

"It's the least I could do."

"It's too bad we're not Eskimos, Dennis. Then you could take me out on the ice and leave me there and come back in and have a scotch and it would all be a lot easier."

"Do you need more tablets?"

"Not yet."

It grew quiet and Terry dozed off and Dennis took his scotch and went out through the kitchen door into the garden. It was pitch black, the night sky over the vale was luminous and he stood sucking in the cold air. He put the glass on the sill next to the door and, unbuttoning his trousers, urinated into the flower bed. In the darkness beyond was the garden shed and Dennis remembered standing there with Terry long ago, both of them drunk, pissing into Sharon's garden. Terry had told a story about the shed. "This is Keeper's Cottage," he had said. "The game keepers for the manor house lived here. And that was the shed where they kept their dogs. They were drunk and they sent the boy out to feed the dogs and the next morning they found what was left of him. Dogs ate him."

"You made that up," Dennis had said.

"No. God's truth. Sometimes you can hear those dogs and the boy screaming."

"Bullshit!"

"God's truth," and Terry had slipped back into the accent of his boyhood, the two of them standing there, swaying in the dark and Dennis remembered Terry saying, "Tuck your willie back in, Dennis. You don't want some ghost dog nipping it off."

Dennis went back into the house and wrapped himself in a blanket on the couch opposite Terry who was sleeping in the chair.

He awoke at first light, listening to the birds in the woods next door and when David arrived, Dennis had made breakfast for himself, and a soft boiled egg for Terry and there was fresh coffee on the stove. He telephoned the number that David found for him and arranged for a taxi to take him up to Heathrow. It would cost a hundred pounds, but it would save time. He would be picked up at the house at six the next morning and dropped off at the terminal two hours later. Terry was unconscious most of the day, and Dennis wandered around the house, leafing through Terry's books, walking down the lane to the pub, having a beer and coming back to spend most of the afternoon napping in a chair on the lawn. Once he awoke to find David spreading a blanket over his shoulders.

The following morning the taxi arrived and Dennis said goodbye to David, who had spent the night. Terry was unconscious and Dennis touched his shoulders, bent to kiss his forehead and left.

A hour later the sun came up, a red ball that hung momentarily on the horizon before rising steadily in the mist.

"There's Windsor over there, sir," the driver said. "Queen's at home, she is. Flag's flying."

Dennis had a window seat, something he requested when he flew alone, since it meant that he could lean against the bulkhead and sleep. Exhausted, he jammed a pillow behind his head, pulled the shade and immediately was unconscious. Hours later he awoke to find the cabin in darkness, passengers sleeping or watching the tiny television screens in the seat backs facing them. He managed to get out of his seat, lifting himself over the sleeping man next to him and went to the toilet where he splashed water on his face, got a drink of juice from the stewardesses who were talking behind closed curtains in the galley. He walked the length of the aisle several times, getting the kinks out of his legs, then returned to his seat, careful to avoid the legs of his sleeping seatmate. When he had settled into his seat he cracked the shade a bit, and looked out.

What he saw was startling. Below were white mountains, brilliant in the sun, their collapsed volcanic peaks like black holes, ridges in such sharp relief that they looked like knife edges. The sun was low, slanting at the stark landscape and he watched as they moved over mountains, glaciers that spilled out into blue-green ice moraines. Then the landscape began to flatten, and there were nothing but sheets of ice, fading to a horizon that was indistinct, the bone-white of the ice blending into the blue-white of the sky. Rivers of cracks appeared in the ice, pale blue lines that crazed the surface.

He thought about the people who must live in such a landscape, and marveled at how a human being could survive. He thought of polar bears and seals coming up through the ice, and watched closely, wondering if, at 30,000 feet, one could see a polar bear on the ice below.

He thought of Terry's words about being put out on the ice to die. He imagined Terry's gaunt frame sitting on one of those sheets, facing the blinding sun, and he watched, fascinated, as the plane moved across a whiteness that seemed to have no end.

He did not know how long he had been watching the arctic ice when he felt a tap on his shoulder. It was a stewardess, bent over the sleeping man next to him.

"Sir," she said. "Would you mind lowering your shade? There are people trying to sleep."

Dennis looked past her at the people in the middle section. One woman was staring at him and he realized that she had probably been the one who had pressed the call button.

"It's beautiful," Dennis said. "I've never seen anything like it in my whole life."

"Yes. But there are people who would like to sleep."

"They should be looking at this. In their whole lives they won't see anything else like it. They can sleep when they get home. They can watch TV to their heart's content. They can't afford to miss this."

Dennis realized that she had looked out the window dozens of times on dozens of flights, and he remembered flying over the pole countless times in the last twenty years of going to and from England, but somehow the scene that he had been watching was different. There was a luminosity and a desolation that was frighteningly wonderful.

"If you'd like to come to the rear of the aircraft, there's a window in the emergency door that you can look through." She said it as if he were a first-time flyer who ought to be humored, but he knew she wasn't going to go away while the woman across the aisle continued to glare.

"No," Dennis said. "I understand." He pulled the shade down. The woman across the aisle looked smug. A few minutes later he pulled the blanket up around his shoulders, stretched it across the bottom of the window and raised the shade so that he could look at the earth passing below without letting light cross the aisle. The ice sheets were broken by thousands of tiny frozen lakes now and as they moved steadily south the ice gave way to patches of snow-covered plain. I have left Terry on the ice floe, Dennis thought. He will die and there will be a memorial service and I will not be there, but Claire and I will come back to England in the Fall and see some plays in London and drive down to Dorset and perhaps have dinner with David and his family. We will drink wine and eat well and we'll take long walks along the lanes and everyone will say how much they miss Terry, but the fact is that Terry is gone. He was here, and now he's gone.

And then Dennis remembered a Cavafy poem that he had taught to his students. It was a small poem, one that they responded well to about a lover who had disappeared. It ended with the lines,

"Memory, keep them the way they were.

And, memory, whatever of that love you can bring back, whatever you can, bring back tonight."

Terry would have known that poem in Greek, not in English, Dennis thought. Claire would be waiting at the airport. He wished he had bought the glass heart.

The Swimmer

The heat was intolerable. She came down the path to the beach, picking her way over the stones, and when she came to the bottom of the path she draped her towel over the broken slab of concrete, and carefully moved across the rocky beach toward the water. The hotel was high above her, and there were whitewashed houses clinging to the cliffs above the cove but the beach was empty except for two men who lay on towels about twenty yards off. She could feel them watching her as she stepped out of her sandals and waded into the water

It was cool and before her the intense blue green stretched toward a cloudless horizon. She slipped into the water and pushed off, breast-stroking until she was beyond the lapping waves. Each stroke brought water to her face and her skin tingled.

She turned on her back and floated for a few seconds. She could still see the two men on the beach and she turned on her stomach and began to swim again, this time with even strokes that took her out into deeper water, the green turning to inky blue. For some reason she kept swimming, far beyond the limit she usually set for herself, stroking steadily, her head in the water, turning occasionally to suck in air, pulling strongly with each stroke. When she finally paused, treading water, she revolved until she faced the shore. The hotel was tiny and the men were no longer visible. The swell was noticeable at this distance, and she realized that she was outside the cove, just in the open sea and there was a brief moment of panic. But the water was buoyant and it felt good and she bobbed in the sea, and then she reached up and pulled the shoulder strap of her bathing suit down over her arm, first one, then the other until her suit was bunched at her waist. She floated a few seconds longer, and then, effortlessly, she slipped the suit down over her hips, pulling it free and she was naked in the sea, the suit in one hand. She could see it in the clear water and she wondered what she would do with it and then, as if it were the most natural thing to do, she let go and watched it drift down until she could no longer see it and she was treading water naked.

She dove, pulling herself down with powerful strokes, searching for her suit but it was gone and she came back toward the luminous surface, bursting into the air, gasping for breath. Looking down into the water she could see her breasts, no longer flat against her chest, but moving in the water, as if they, too, were floating and she reached down and stroked her naked stomach. She turned on her back and floated, and for the next half hour she alternately swam a few strokes and floated, feeling the sun on her face and then on her shoulders, until, growing tired, she turned toward the shore.

The hotel grew in size until she could see the terraces and the two men on their towels grew larger and she wondered how she would get back to the room. She remembered an old joke from her childhood about the dumbest boy in school who was told to take a note to the girls' physical education teacher. He knocked on the door of the girls' locker room and called out, "Close your eyes girls, I'm coming in."

Perhaps if she closed her eyes she wouldn't see anyone, and she would be invisible and she could walk naked up the path and across the narrow street to the hotel and through the lobby and no one would see her.

She came to the shallow water, put her feet on the rocky bottom and rose, her body coming out of the water and she remembered the frieze in the museum in Florence with Neptune surrounded by his mermaids. The two men rose to their elbows, watching her. She continued out of the water, finding her sandals, slipping her feet into them, carefully making her way across the rocky beach to where her towel lay across the slab.

But she didn't pull the towel around her body. She picked it up and started up the path, feeling the humid air on her skin, the coolness of evaporating water and she climbed until she came to the street. She went between the parked cars, crossed the street, unconscious of the pedestrians who turned their heads to watch the slender naked woman carrying a towel enter the door of the hotel.

At the desk she paused. The desk clerk turned and stared at her. He cannot see me, she thought. How will he know to give me my key. She waited.

"Are you all right, miss?" he said.

Apparently he was speaking to someone else. She waited.

"Miss?"

She said nothing. There was nothing to be said any more.

He reached back, took a key from one of the boxes and, placing it on the counter, slid it toward her. His eyes were fixed on her breasts.

She picked up the key, turned and went toward the tiny lift with the wrought iron gates. There was an older couple already in the lift, the English pair that she had seen earlier arguing with the desk clerk about something in their room that was broken. They looked at her and then they both fixed their eyes on the doorway to the lift. She pulled the gate closed and touched the button for her floor and the lift started with a jerk, creaking back and forth as it slowly rose. She could hear the intake of breath from the woman. When the lift stopped with a jolt she opened the gate and stepped out and made her way to her room, sandals flapping against the tiles.

Inside the room it was dark and she opened the shutters, letting the afternoon heat flood into the room. Her skin felt clammy and she stood in the opening, hoping that some tiny breath of wind would come up. Roger was not back yet from the Monastery of the Virgin. Roger liked churches and shrines. She took one of his neatly pressed white shirts from a hanger and put it on and lay on the bed. Tonight they would have supper at a trattoria where she could watch the sea.

Acknowledgment: Madelaine Cooke for advice on the design of the back cover.